The

by Margaret K. and Charles M. Wetterer
illustrations by Mary O'Keefe Young

Carolrhoda Books, Inc./Minneapolis

JF
Wett

For Kate and Anna Wetterer and their parents
—C. M. W. and M. K. W.

For my father and favorite historian, Richard O'Keefe
—M. O'K. Y.

The authors wish to thank the staffs of Huntington (New York) Public Library and Center Moriches (New York) Public Library; the New York Historical Society; and Mr. B. Gene Badlato, former Chief Building Inspector for New York City, who helped retrace Milton's route. Special thanks to Mrs. Hazel Daub Saville, Milton's daughter, who provided many homey details of her father's family.

Text copyright © 1996 by Charles M. and Margaret K. Wetterer
Illustrations copyright © 1996 by Carolrhoda Books, Inc.

This book is available in two editions:
Library binding by Carolrhoda Books, Inc.
Soft cover by First Avenue Editions
c/o The Lerner Group
241 First Avenue North, Minneapolis, Minnesota 55401

Library of Congress Cataloging-in-Publication Data

Wetterer, Charles M.
    The snow walker / by Charles M. Wetterer and Margaret
  K. Wetterer ; illustrations by Mary O'Keefe Young.
      p. cm.—(Carolrhoda on my own books)
    ISBN 0-87614-891-7 (lib. bdg.)
    ISBN 0-87614-959-X (pbk.)
    1. Blizzards—New York (N.Y.)—History—19th century—
  Juvenile literature. 2. New York (N.Y.)—History—1865–
  1898—Juvenile literature. 3. Daub, Milton—Juvenile
  literature. 4. Bronx (New York, N.Y.)—History—Juvenile
  literature. [1. Blizzards—New York (N.Y.) 2. New York
  (N.Y.)—History—1865–1898. 3. Daub, Milton.] I. Wetterer,
  Margaret K. II. Young, Mary O'Keefe, ill. III. Title.
  IV. Series: Carolrhoda on my own book.
  F128.47.W49 1995
  974.7'275—dc20   94-44131
                                                       CIP
                                                        AC

Manufactured in the United States of America
1 2 3 4 5 6 JR 01 00 99 98 97 96

Author's Note

For three days in March 1888, a blizzard raged throughout the northeastern United States. Snow and ice buried the land from Maine to Maryland. Roads were closed, and hundreds of passenger trains were stuck for days behind huge snowdrifts. Winds, some over 80 miles per hour, cracked windows, tore away fences, roofs, and signs, and toppled trees and utility poles. Thousands of birds fell frozen from bushes and buildings where they had huddled for shelter. Miles of telephone and telegraph wires snapped under the pressure of wind, ice, and snow. Cities and towns, farms and families were cut off from one another. For a time, the government, in Washington, D.C., lost all contact with the rest of the country. At sea, violent winds and waves damaged countless boats and sank more than two hundred of them.

Milton Daub was 12 years old when the storm struck. He and his family lived in the Bronx, a town that had become part of New York City a few years before. At the time, the Bronx had a small business and residential center with miles of fields and farms to the north. The Daubs' two-story wooden frame house faced 145th Street, a wide dirt road. Milton was the oldest of five children. He had two sisters, Ella and Hannah, and two little brothers, Maurice and Jerome.

This is the story of Milton Daub's adventure in that terrible storm, known ever after as the Blizzard of '88.

Monday, March 12, 1888

Crack!

The sound jolted Milton awake.

A howling wind rattled the window.

Milton jumped out of bed
and pushed aside the curtains.

A smile lit his face. Snow!

Snow was everywhere.

He saw that a giant branch had broken
from the maple tree.

Now wind was tossing it crazily
across the yard.

Quickly Milton pulled on his school clothes
and ran downstairs.
Snow covered all the windows.
The hall and parlor were dark.
Back in the kitchen,
Mama had lit the kerosene lamp.
Everyone was eating breakfast,
even baby Jerome in his high chair.

"Mama! Why didn't you call me?"
Milton asked.

"It's after 7:30. I'll be late for school."

"No school today," his mother replied.

"There's a wall of snow
blocking the front door."

"We'll all stay home," said his father.

"It's dangerous out in that storm."

"We have plenty of food," Mama said,
checking the icebox.
"But I do wish we had more milk."
"I'll go and buy some," Milton offered.
"Don't be foolish, Milton!"
his father exclaimed.
"The drifts are already climbing
to the second story.
You would be buried out there."
"I could go on snowshoes," Milton insisted.

"And where are you going to get
snowshoes?" his father asked.
"We could make some," Milton replied.
"At school, we've been studying
the Alaska Territory.
There are pictures of snowshoes
in my geography book.
I bet we could make a pair.
Could we try, Papa? Please?"
His father laughed. "All right, son.
Eat your oatmeal," he said.
"Then we'll try
to make you some snowshoes."

After breakfast, Milton and his father
set to work.
They used wooden barrel hoops, thin slats,
wire, heavy cord, and the bottom
of an old pair of roller skates
with the wheels off.
Finally, after almost two hours,
the snowshoes were ready to try out.

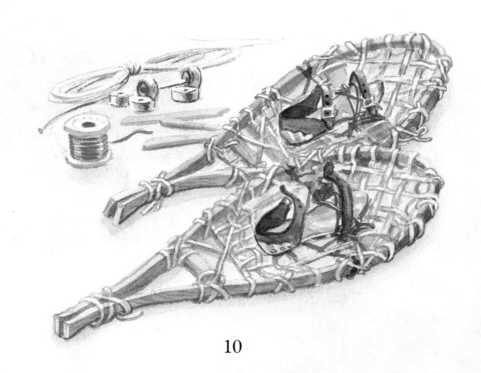

Everyone crowded into
the little upstairs bedroom.
Milton piled on sweaters, an overcoat,
a wool hat, a scarf, and mittens.
His father helped him
strap on the snowshoes.
Then he tied a rope around his son's waist.
"Okay, Milton. I'll hold onto the line
until we're sure
your snowshoes work," he said.
"If you start to sink, I'll pull you back."
He opened the window.
An icy wind swept snow into the room.
The girls shrieked.
Mama covered Jerome with her shawl.

Milton pulled his hat down over his ears
and his scarf up over his mouth.
He wished he had an Alaskan parka.
He took one step,
then a second, and a third.
He had to keep his feet apart.
Otherwise, he stepped one snowshoe
on the other, and couldn't walk.
Milton climbed up and down the snowdrift
to the window several times.
At last, his father nodded.
The snowshoes worked.
Milton untied the clothesline.
His father handed him a sled
with a wooden box nailed to it.
"Watch for landmarks
so you don't get lost," Papa warned.
"Please be careful," his mother called.

Milton leaned into the biting wind.
He snowshoed across the front yard
and over the garden fence.
Wind had swept the road clear
to an icy base in some places.
In others, Milton had to climb
over drifts of snow.
Some drifts were as hard as icebergs.
Some moved beneath his feet.
At times, gusts of wind
scooped up fallen snow
and tossed it back into the air.

When that happened, Milton saw nothing,
only whiteness swirling around him.
He hardly recognized the houses he passed.
Everything looked so different
piled with snow and hung with icicles.

Milton reached the spot where he knew
Mike Ash's grocery store should be.
At first, he couldn't find it.
The sign had blown away,
and snow covered the door and window.
Then he climbed up the snowdrift
and tapped on the window
of the Ashes' apartment above the store.
He held onto the window ledge
to keep from being blown away.
Mr. Ash opened the window a crack.
"Milton! What are you doing out
in this storm?" he yelled above the wind.

"How did you get up here?"
his son Mickey wanted to know.
"My mother needs milk, Mr. Ash,"
Milton shouted back with a grin.
"Like my snowshoes, Mickey?"
"No fresh milk was delivered today,
Milton," said the grocer.
"But I can sell you condensed milk."

Milton gave him fifty cents.

Mr. Ash went downstairs to the store.

He returned with five cans of milk.

Mickey leaned out the window

for a better look at Milton's snowshoes.

Quickly, Mr. Ash pulled him back in

and shut the window.

Milton tugged his scarf up over his face
and started for home.

A neighbor who was watching
from her upstairs window shouted,
"Young man, can I buy some of that milk?"
Milton sold her a can of milk.
He asked for ten cents,
but the woman insisted he take a quarter.
Another neighbor called to him.
Then another.

Soon Milton had sold all the cans of milk.
He snowshoed back to Mr. Ash's store
and bought more condensed milk.
But again, at almost every house he passed,
someone shouted for milk.

As he dragged his sled back to Ash's store,
Milton pictured the dogsleds of Alaska.
Maybe he and his father
could make a dogsled, he thought.

When he got back to the store,
he bought a whole case of milk
with the extra money people had
given him.
He sold this milk, and then another case,
to neighbors.
By now, half the kids in the neighborhood
had seen and admired his snowshoes.

Milton grinned when he thought of
how surprised they would be
if he came by on a dogsled.
He imagined himself
and all the dogs of the neighborhood
out in the storm,
and all the rest of the world snowed in.

Just then, the noon whistle
blew at the factory.
Milton was surprised.
He didn't feel as if he had been out
for almost two hours.
He set out for home at once.
Snow clung to his clothes like lint.
Snowflakes driven by the wind
stung and reddened his eyes and nose.
His toes ached from the cold.
But Milton felt like cheering
as he snowshoed home,
pulling the sled after him.

Back at home, Milton's father helped him in
through the bedroom window.

"What took you so long?" he asked.

"We've been frantic with worry,"
his mother exclaimed.

"I'm sorry, Mama. I've been getting milk
for our neighbors," said Milton.

He pulled coins and bills from his pockets.

"Milton! How much did you charge them?"
his mother asked.

"Ten cents," he said.

"But people kept giving me more."

After lunch, Milton begged to go out again.

"Honestly, Mama, I won't go far," he said.

"It's great fun.

And there are many more people who

need milk.

With these snowshoes, Papa, I'm safe."

Papa looked at Mama.

"All right," he agreed after a minute.

"The snowshoes seem to be holding up well.

But be home well before dark.

Five o'clock at the latest."

"Milton, put these on," said Mama.

She handed him three pairs

of wool stockings.

"I don't want your feet to get frostbitten."

Milton had to wear a pair
of his father's old shoes to fit
over all those stockings.
Bundled up, Milton stepped again
through the window and into the blizzard.
In his imagination, he was back in Alaska.

By three o'clock,
Milton had bought
and sold all the milk
in Mr. Ash's store.
He decided to go to Roach's grocery,
four blocks away on Willis Avenue.
On the way, Milton passed
empty horse wagons and carriages.
They were almost buried in snow.
He cut across the road to avoid
a broken telegraph pole that swung wildly
from wires over the street.

Didn't Alaskans on their lonely travels
sometimes face danger too? he thought.
Didn't they have to watch out for
wolves and polar bears?
Snow covered Roach's grocery store.
Mr. Roach was surprised to see Milton
outside his apartment window.
But he brought up a case of milk
from the grocery store
and sold it through the window.

As Milton pulled the sled over a snowdrift,
he felt his right snowshoe loosen.
A couple of the wires had snapped.
With icy fingers,
he twisted them onto unbroken wires.
He would finish selling this case of milk,
he decided, then head for home
before the snowshoe came apart.

Milton sold the last of the milk.

Then a woman called to him

from a third-floor window.

"Sonny," she said, "would you please

go to the drugstore for me?

My husband is sick. He needs medicine."

She threw down a slip of paper

held by a clothespin.

It spun in the wind,

and Milton grabbed for it.

It was a doctor's prescription.

He would get the medicine, he told himself,

and then go straight home.

"Wait," the woman called.

"I'll give you some money."

Milton didn't wait.

He didn't think about his broken snowshoe.

He headed for McKane's drugstore.

Mrs. McKane was shocked to see Milton
peering over the windowsill
of the apartment above the store.
She called her husband.
He took the prescription
and hurried downstairs.

Soon, he came back with a small package.
"Get this to the sick man
as soon as possible," he urged.
"How much does it cost?" asked Milton.
"No charge," Mr. McKane replied.
"Anyone who comes out in a storm like this
doesn't have to pay for medicine."

Milton made his way
back to the woman's house.
He felt his right snowshoe flapping again.
Another wire had broken.
I have to get home, he thought nervously.
Without snowshoes,
I might sink into snow over my head.
I might freeze in a snowdrift.
The woman whose husband needed
medicine was watching for Milton.

She lowered a can on a string
so he could send up the package.
"How much was the medicine?" she called.
"No charge," he shouted back.
A woman from the apartment below
opened a window.
"Young man," she pleaded,
"would you please go to the store for me?
We have no food in the house."
All right, Milton thought.
I will get the food for this lady
and *then* go home.

Milton took the shopping list and money.
He headed back to Roach's store.
He twisted his scarf
so that only his eyes showed.
Still, as he pushed
through the waves of snow,
icy bits blew in.
They stung his nose and cheeks.
He thought of the woman
and her sick husband.
Did they need food too?

"Please fill this order
for a lady down the street," said Milton.
"And, Mr. Roach, would you make up
the same order for me?"
When Milton delivered the groceries,
the woman told him to keep the change.
"Thank you," he said.
"This bag of groceries
is for the lady upstairs.
Tell her I hope her husband gets better."
"God bless you, son. I will,"
the woman said.

By this time, it was after four o'clock.

Milton tried to hurry home.

But now both snowshoes were wobbling.

The left one had a few broken wires.

He could twist them back onto the slats.

But his right snowshoe was coming apart.

He stepped as lightly on it as he could.

Soon his legs ached

with every awkward step.

Even with three pairs of stockings,

his toes felt icy.

A frozen bird fell from a tree

and landed on his shoulder.

Milton jumped, stepping hard

on his right snowshoe.

Another wire snapped.

Suddenly, Milton was afraid.

He was alone.

He had not seen one other person
out in the storm.

What if he sank into a drift
and disappeared?

No one would know he was there.

A violent gust of wind
flung up a cloud of fallen snow.
For several seconds,
Milton could barely see or breathe.
It was getting dark.
Where exactly was he?
He had to get home.
He trudged on.
He couldn't move fast enough
to keep warm.
He was beginning to get chilled.

Finally, Milton recognized his own street.

Just ahead was his house.

His spirits soared. He felt like an Alaskan returning from a dangerous journey.

He glimpsed his sister Hannah's red hair at a window.

Then he saw the whole family.

They smiled and waved.

At last, Milton struggled up the snowdrift
to the bedroom window.
Mr. Daub lifted him over the sill
and pulled the sled in after him.
"You look exhausted, son," he said.
"Yes, Papa, I am," Milton replied.
He emptied his pockets of coins and bills
and proudly handed them to his mother.
Papa unstrapped the snowshoes.
"Thank God you're home safe," said Mama,
looking at the broken snowshoes.
"I should never have let you go."

They helped Milton pull off
his snow-covered clothes.
He put on his nightshirt and got into bed.
Mama brought him a hot supper.
Milton ate only a bit.
Then he fell asleep,
even though it was only six o'clock.
Snow continued to fall all that night
and through the next day.
Finally, on Wednesday, the storm was over.
People in the South Bronx dug out
from under mountains of snow.

They all talked about
the boy who had walked on snow
through the blizzard
to help his neighbors.
Many people stopped by the house
to thank Milton.
One woman could not thank him enough.
Milton had not only given her milk
and much-needed food, she declared.
Milton had helped save her husband's life.

Afterword

The 1888 blizzard set records that have not been broken even after more than a hundred years. The northeastern United States has never again seen such a huge snowfall over such a large area. Wind speed, snow levels, and low temperature records for dozens of places in the area still stand. Besides the many people who suffered from frostbite, exhaustion, and injuries from falls, more than four hundred people died during the storm. Never before or since has a blizzard in the United States taken so many lives. Stories of the storm became part of American folklore.

Milton Daub, his family, and his neighbors never forgot his snow-walking during the great Blizzard of '88.